Home Is The Sailor

Terry Denton

For Liz and Roy

Houghton Mifflin Company
Boston 1989

Claude and Sparky lived by the sea.

Each day the two friends would sail their little boat in the quiet bay. Claude often felt restless, and wanted to know what lay beyond the lighthouses. Sparky was more of a stay-at-home type, who felt worried every time Claude brought out the maps and charts.

One blazing summer's afternoon
Claude was feeling hot. He
decided to set sail for the North,
where it would be cooler. Sparky
suggested they spend the day
with a good book and glasses of icy
lemonade. However, Claude was
determined to go, and steered the
little boat out of the bay. Sparky
sulked for a while, but cheered up
when he felt the cooler breezes
brush his beak.

As the twilight grew, Claude spotted a glowing light bobbing gently on the waves. Who could this be?

"Captain Hagar, at your service," announced the old seal as Claude and Sparky drew near. "While I am immensely wise in the ways of the sea, I seem to be lost on this, my last great voyage. And also I have misplaced my spectacles." He paused to look more closely at the young boy and the little penguin. "Would you gentlemen be so kind as to assist me home?"

Claude looked into the old seal's sad eyes and said, "Of course we will."

And so they set sail for the North.
Claude and Sparky steered the
little boat while the Captain slept.

But as night fell a great storm
arose.

The wind howled and the waves became huge. Claude and Sparky were so frightened they hugged each other very tight as the little boat was flung about the waves.

Captain Hagar stumbled from his deep sleep. "You chaps having a bit of trouble?"

The Captain took firm hold of the rudder, and with Claude's help guided the little boat to safer waters.

Claude and Sparky were so relieved they danced a jig that Sparky had learned at Ms. Fairweather's School for Dancing Sailors.

Then it was morning, and Sparky made hot chocolate and pancakes with honey for breakfast. Captain Hagar politely declined his share. "I must watch my diet, you know, ha ha," he said, patting his ample stomach. "A couple of sardines will do me nicely, thank you so much."

After sailing north for much of the day, the most wonderful lights appeared on the horizon.

"The Land of the Midnight Sea! My home!" boomed the Captain joyfully. And there in front of them was a great city, all made of ice.

Claude stole a look at the Captain. Tears were glistening on his furry cheeks.

Captain Hagar steered the little boat through the center of the city toward a bustling marketplace.

Claude and Sparky then accompanied the Captain to a modest but friendly house. "Here I will live out the rest of my days," he said. The residents greeted the Captain with joy, and welcomed his new friends inside.

After a first-rate fish dinner, the old sailors sang sea chanteys. The Captain joined them in his rich bass voice. Encouraged by Claude, Sparky danced for the applauding audience.

The next day Claude and Sparky prepared for their journey home. As they were about to leave, the Captain presented Claude with his hat, compass, sextant, and maps.

"You are now a master of the sea," he said.

Claude and Sparky said farewell to the Captain, and set their course for the South.

As they sailed on in the crisp bright morning, they found themselves wending their way through a bewildering number of icebergs. After a while Claude realized they had struck an ice maze.

However, Claude now had the
compass, sextant, and maps, and
he worked out a path through the
maze while Sparky took care of
the sails.

After sailing all day, the two friends caught sight of the familiar welcoming lights of their bay. Soon they were home, on dry land.

Claude and Sparky celebrated their safe return with tall glasses of lemonade.

Claude just smiled when Sparky complained that it had gone flat and warm.

"Next time," Claude said, "remember to leave it in the fridge."

*The author would like to thank Rita Scharf of
Oxford University Press for guiding this book to
calm waters.*

Library of Congress Cataloging-in-Publication Data

Denton, Terry.
    Home is the sailor / Terry Denton. — 1st American ed.
      p.   cm.
    "Originally published in Australia in 1988 by Oxford University
Press"—T.p. verso.
    Summary: A young boy and his penguin friend set sail to find
cooler waters and meet a stranded old sailor in search of the Land
of the Midnight Sea.
    ISBN 0-395-51525-4
    [1. Sailing—Fiction. 2. Sea stories.] I. Title.
PZ7.D4374Ho   1989   89-1822
[E]—dc19   CIP
                 AC

Printed in Hong Kong

10 9 8 7 6 5 4 3 2 1